Oz

THE GREAT AND POWERFUL

THE WITCHES OF OZ

ADAPTED BY SCOTT PETERSON AND MICHAEL SIGLAIN
BASED ON THE SCREENPLAY BY MITCHELL KAPNER AND DAVID LINDSAY-ABAIRE
BASED ON THE BOOKS OF L. FRANK BAUM

EXECUTIVE PRODUCERS GRANT CURTIS, PALAK PATEL, PHILIP STEUER, JOSH DONEN
PRODUCED BY JOE ROTH
SCREEN STORY BY MITCHELL KAPNER
SCREENPLAY BY MITCHELL KAPNER AND DAVID LINDSAY-ABAIRE
DIRECTED BY SAM RAIMI

DISNEP PRESS
NEW YORK

Printed in the United States of America

First Edition

1 3 5 7 9 10 8 6 4 2

G658-7729-4-12349

ISBN 978-1-4231-7089-1

For more Disney Press fun, visit www.disneybooks.com.

For more Oz fun, visit www.disney.com/thewizard.

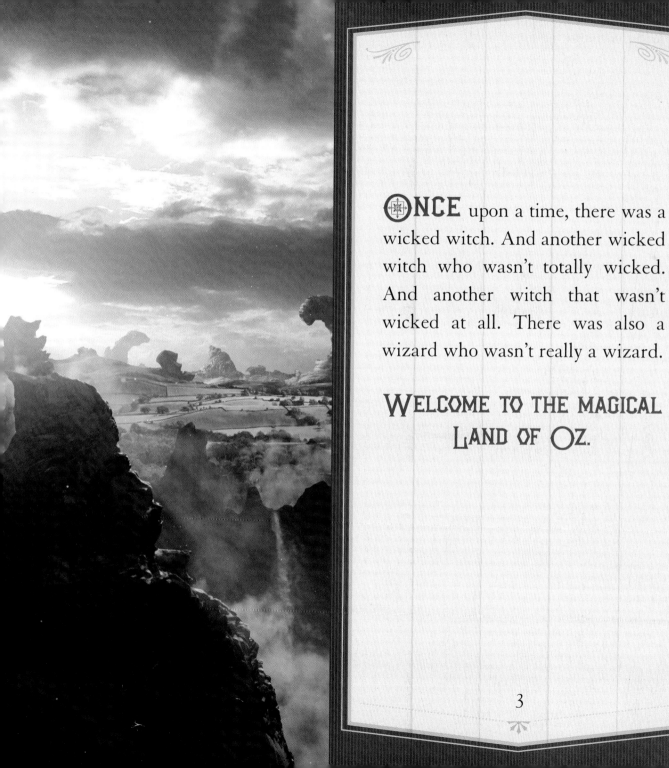

ONCE upon a time, there was a wicked witch. And another wicked witch who wasn't totally wicked. And another witch that wasn't wicked at all. There was also a wizard who wasn't really a wizard.

WELCOME TO THE MAGICAL LAND OF OZ.

THE WIZARD who wasn't a wizard was a man from Kansas named Oscar, but people called him Oz. He wasn't a wizard, but he *was* a magician—a good one. Unfortunately, he wasn't always a good man.

After some of his tricks got him into trouble, Oz escaped in a hot-air balloon. But when his balloon got caught in a tornado, it carried him to a faraway land unlike any he had ever seen.

THE MAGICAL LAND was also called Oz. There, Oz met Theodora, who was a witch.

Oz didn't believe witches were real. He also thought that if there were any real witches, they'd be ugly. And mean.

But Theodora really was a witch. And she had magic powers, like the ability to shoot fire from her hands. She was also really pretty, and she really liked Oz, whom she mistook for a great and powerful wizard.

OZ DECIDED that he really liked being Oz in Oz, so Theodora introduced him to the land and the good people of Oz.

He met all kinds of people and creatures, like the tall Winkie soldiers and Finley, a flying monkey. Oz saved Finley from a lion. After that, the two became good friends.

Theodora brought Oz and Finley to the Emerald City, where Oz would become king. But first, he had to meet Theodora's big sister, Evanora.

EVANORA WAS A WITCH, TOO and she had the power

to shoot electricity from her fingertips. Evanora was also beautiful—very beautiful.

But unlike Theodora, Evanora wasn't quite so young. And unlike Theodora, Evanora didn't really trust Oz. Evanora knew that Oz wasn't really a wizard.

Evanora didn't tell Oz that she knew the truth about him. Instead, she played along and pretended that he really was the great and powerful Oz.

IN ORDER FOR OZ to become king, he had to defeat another witch—the Wicked Witch.

Oz was trapped. He was afraid to admit he wasn't a wizard. But he was also afraid to fight a wicked witch.

Evanora gave him no choice. So off Oz went to fight the Wicked Witch.

He took Finley the monkey with him. On the way, they passed through China Town. There, they met China Girl, who was small and fragile but smart. Oz helped her, and she joined the quest.

BUT WHEN they found the Witch, Oz couldn't bring himself to strike.

It wasn't just that the Wicked Witch was beautiful—although she was. And it wasn't just that he wasn't actually a wizard—although he wasn't.

It was that, to his surprise, deep down, Oz really was a good person. Good thing, then, that the "Wicked" Witch was actually a good witch.

IT HAD ALL BEEN A TRICK. The Witch's name was Glinda. Of the three Witches, she was actually the only good one. Glinda had a powerful magic wand and used it to fly inside a giant, clear bubble.

Glinda cared deeply for the people of Oz and wanted to see them free from Evanora, who was the real Wicked Witch. The only way to stop her was for Glinda to team up with Oz.

But there was one other person in their way—THEODORA.

THEODORA WAS YOUNG,

confused, and heartbroken that Oz has joined forces with Glinda.

Evanora convinced her sister that it would be better to be wicked and have no heart at all than to be good and have a heart that could break. Evanora gave her sister a potion, and soon, Theodora transformed from a beautiful girl into a frightening, green-skinned witch.

THEODORA WAS NOW THE WICKED WITCH OF THE WEST!

TOGETHER, THE WICKED WITCHES unleashed their flying baboons upon the Land of Oz in an attempt to rule over all. But Glinda was not about to let the good people of Oz down, and an epic battle ensued.

But the battle was fought without Oz. No one knew where he was! Glinda didn't know if he was going to help the Land of Oz or try to escape. And just when it seemed all hope would be lost, Oz returned —now he was Oz the Great and Powerful.

GLINDA AND OZ had a few tricks up their sleeves. Glinda believed in Oz, and that gave Oz the strength to work with Glinda, Finley, China Girl, the Tinkers and the rest of the good people of Oz to trick the Witches.

They fooled the Witches into believing that Oz was really great and powerful and that his magic was far greater than the Wicked Witches' powers combined.

Frightened, the Witches retreated, vowing to return to fight another day.

THE GOOD PEOPLE OF OZ REJOICED. Glinda

the Good Witch and the Great and Powerful Oz had won and would always be there to protect them and the Land of Oz.